Five reasons why we think you'll love this book!

Winnie and Wilbur
UNDER THE SEA

Wilbur becomes a cat-fish!

Winnie becomes an octopus!

There is so much to spot in every picture.

Wilbur saves the day when Winnie loses her magic wand.

You can take the Winnie and Wilbur challenge:
can you find a fish sticking out its tongue?

Freya

Anushka

Maggie

Bailey

Johannes

Molly

Ashley

Amber

Jun-Yeong

Pablo

Matilda

Marwin

Hasan

Rebecca

Thank you to all these schools for helping with the endpapers:

St Barnabas Primary School, Oxford; St Ebbe's Primary School,
Oxford; Marcham Primary School, Abingdon; St Michael's C.E.
Aided Primary School, Oxford; St Bede's RC Primary School, Jarrow;
The Western Academy, Beijing, China; John King School, Pinxton;
Neston Primary School, Neston; Star of the Sea RC Primary School,
Whitley Bay; José Jorge Letria Primary School, Cascais, Portugal;
Dunmore Primary School, Abingdon; Özel Bahçeşehir İlköğretim
Okulu, Istanbul, Turkey; the International School of Amsterdam, the
Netherlands; Princethorpe Infant School, Birmingham.

For Pat, who loves the sea—V.T.

For Harriet Bayly and her family—K.P.

OXFORD
UNIVERSITY PRESS

Great Clarendon Street, Oxford OX2 6DP

Oxford University Press is a department of the University of
Oxford. It furthers the University's objective of excellence in
research, scholarship, and education by publishing worldwide.
Oxford is a registered trade mark of Oxford University Press in
the UK and in certain other countries

Text copyright © Valerie Thomas 2011
Illustrations copyright © Korky Paul 2011, 2016
The moral rights of the author and artist
have been asserted

Database right Oxford University Press (maker)

First published as *Winnie Under the Sea* in 2011
This edition first published in 2016

British Library Cataloguing in Publication Data available

ISBN: 978-0-19-274831-7 (paperback)
ISBN: 978-0-19-274920-8 (paperback and CD)

10 9 8 7 6 5 4 3 2 1

Printed in China

Paper used in the production of this book is a natural, recyclable
product made from wood grown in sustainable forests.
The manufacturing process conforms to the environmental
regulations of the country of origin

www.winnieandwilbur.com

VALERIE THOMAS AND KORKY PAUL

Winnie and Wilbur
UNDER THE SEA

OXFORD
UNIVERSITY PRESS

It was holiday time for Winnie the Witch
and her big black cat, Wilbur.

'Where will we go this year, Wilbur?' asked Winnie.
She searched the internet and found a little island,
with blue sea, golden sand, and coconut trees.

The bright blue sea was full of beautiful fish.
'Don't the fish look lovely, Wilbur?' she said.
They look delicious, thought Wilbur.
'That's where we'll go,' said Winnie

She packed her suitcase,
Wilbur jumped onto her shoulder,
and they zoomed up into the sky.

At last, there was the island.
It did look lovely.

They landed on the golden sand,
and found a comfortable hut.

Winnie put on her flippers and her goggles,
and dived into the water.

Wilbur climbed a coconut tree.
That was fun.
Then he had a sleep.
That was peaceful.

Winnie was having a lovely time.
The sea was full of fish. There were
dolphins, turtles, and coral.
It was so beautiful.
Winnie wanted Wilbur
to see it, too.

'Wilbur,' called Winnie,
'come and see the fish.
You'll love them!'

Wilbur wanted to see the fish.
He put one paw in the water.
Erk! Nasty! It was wet!
'Meeeeoooow!' cried Wilbur.
He hated getting wet.

GHOTI

Then Winnie had
a wonderful idea.
She waved her
magic wand, shouted,

'Abracadabra!'

and Wilbur was
no longer a cat.

He was a cat-fish!

Wilbur the cat-fish dived
into the waves and swam away.

Winnie watched him through her goggles.

He chased some tiny fish.
Then he dived under a dogfish
and played catch with a crayfish.

Wilbur the cat-fish was having so much fun,
Winnie wanted to be a fish as well.

But she couldn't be a fish.
She had to hold her magic wand.
What could she be?
Of course!

Winnie waved her wand, shouted,

'Abracadabra!'

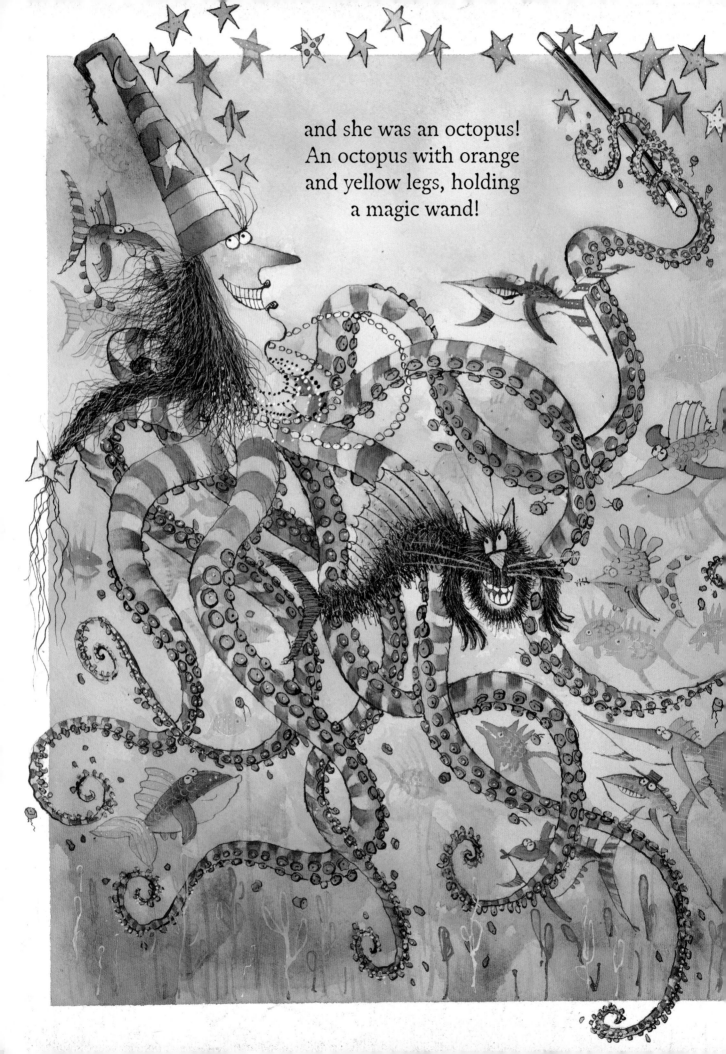

and she was an octopus!
An octopus with orange
and yellow legs, holding
a magic wand!

It was fun being an octopus.
Winnie the octopus waved her eight legs
and floated through the seaweed,
around the coral, over the rocks.

Wilbur the cat-fish darted around her.
Thousands of fish swam with them.
Tiny fish, big fish, and, suddenly . . .

a sea lion.

The sea lion flipped its tail,
and Winnie lost her wand.

She grabbed at it, but missed.

A swordfish tried to spear it for her, but missed.

A jellyfish nearly caught it, but missed.

Down, down it sank,

into the wreck of
an old sailing ship,

and disappeared.

'Blithering broomsticks!' wailed Winnie,
but it sounded like, 'Bubble, bubble, bubble.'
'Bubble, bubble, bubble,' cried Wilbur.

They didn't want to stay under the sea for ever.
Where was the magic wand?
Stuck in the anchor? **No.**

Under the ropes? **No.**   Behind the big crab? **No.**

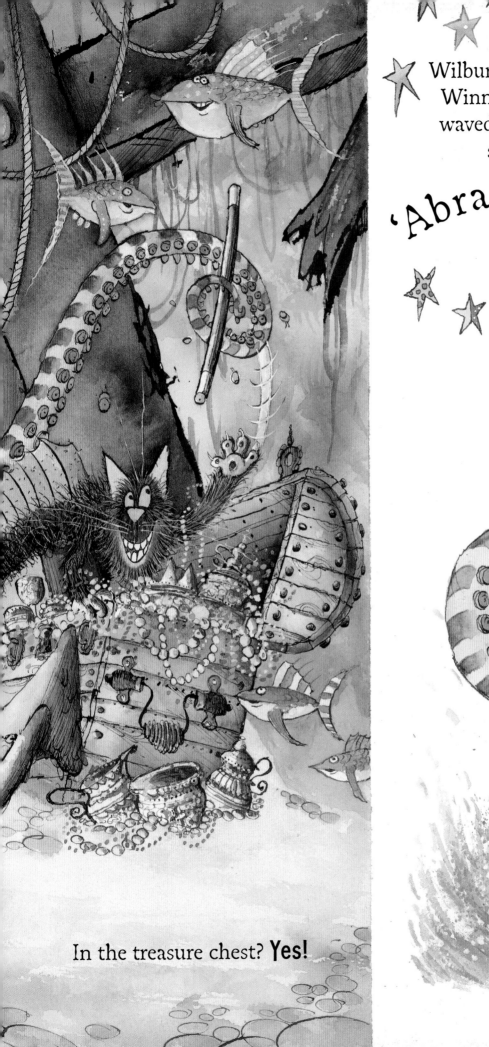

In the treasure chest? **Yes!**

Wilbur flipped it out.
Winnie grabbed it,
waved it five times,
shouted,

'Abracadabra!'

and a **witch** and a **cat** floated back to the shore.

'That was exciting, Wilbur,' Winnie said.
'Too exciting. We won't do that again.
But it is beautiful under the sea.'

Then Winnie had another wonderful idea.

A little yellow boat was bobbing on the waves.
Winnie waved her magic wand, shouted,

GHOTI

'Abracadabra!'

and there, bobbing on the waves . . .

was a yellow submarine.

Winnie and Wilbur went on board.
The fish swam up to the windows and looked in.

'It is lovely under the sea, isn't it Wilbur,' said Winnie.
It's lovely and dry in here, Wilbur thought.
'Purr, purr, purr,' he said.

Bethany

Katia

Eun-Jae

Kathleen

Ji-Eun

Jenny

Sara

Fraser

Ka Keung

Selin

Selin

Olivia

Siyabend

Kieran

A note for grown-ups

Oxford Owl is a FREE and easy-to-use website packed with support and advice about everything to do with reading.

Informative videos

Hints, tips and fun activities

Top tips from top writers for reading with your child

Help with choosing picture books

For this expert advice and much, much more about how children learn to read and how to keep them reading ...

LOOK
for Oxford Owl
www.oxfordowl.co.uk